W9-BRU-346

HUNKY DORY ATE IT

To Jerry, Julie, and Chris

K.E.

For Lynn, Paula, David, Brenda,
and Rebel

J.M.S.

by Katie Evans
pictures by
Janet Morgan Stoeke

A Puffin Unicorn

Clara Lake
baked a cake.

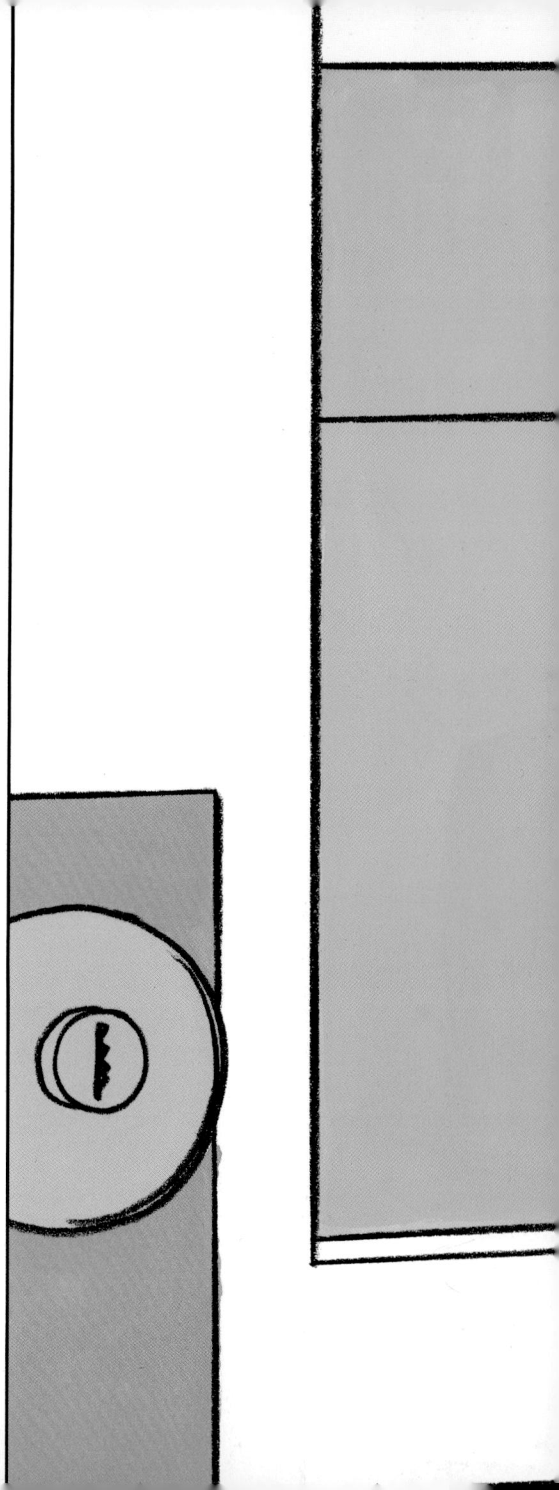

Hunky Dory ate it.

Kate Donetti
boiled spaghetti.

Hunky Dory ate it.

Julie Fry
made a pie.

Hunky Dory ate it.

Sandy Drake
grilled a steak.

Hunky Dory ate it.

Mr. Hart
baked a tart.

Hunky Dory ate it.

Hunky Dory's
stomach dragged.
His sturdy tail
no longer wagged.

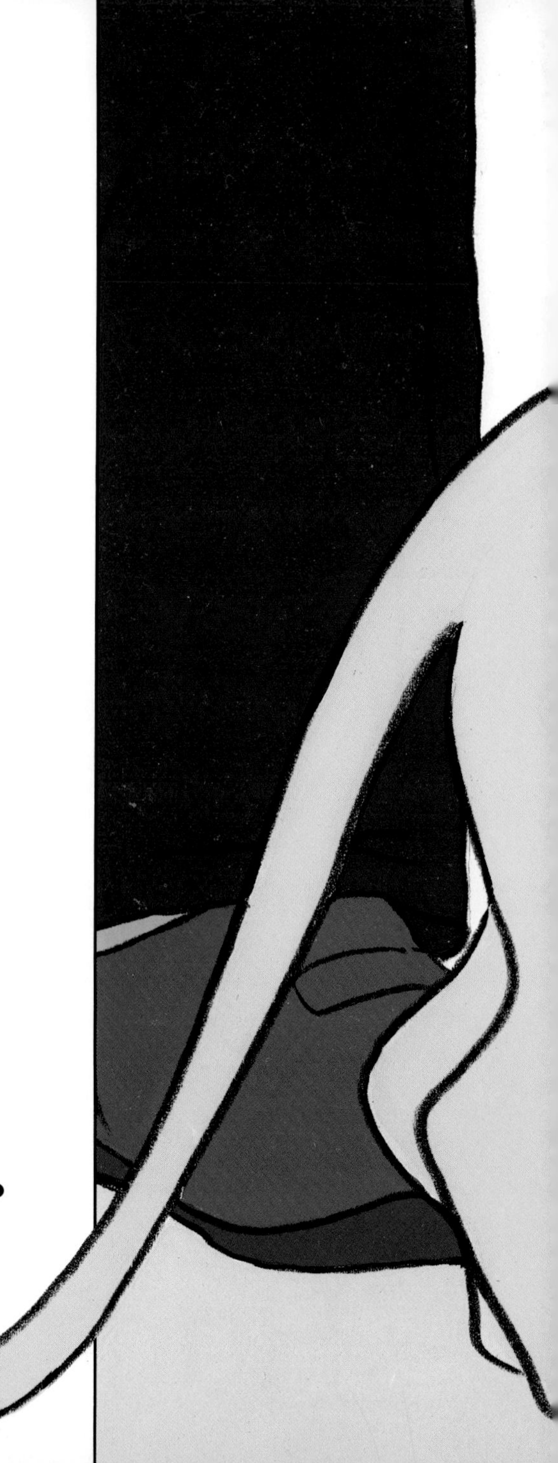

Julie found
her naughty pet.
She quickly took
him to the vet.

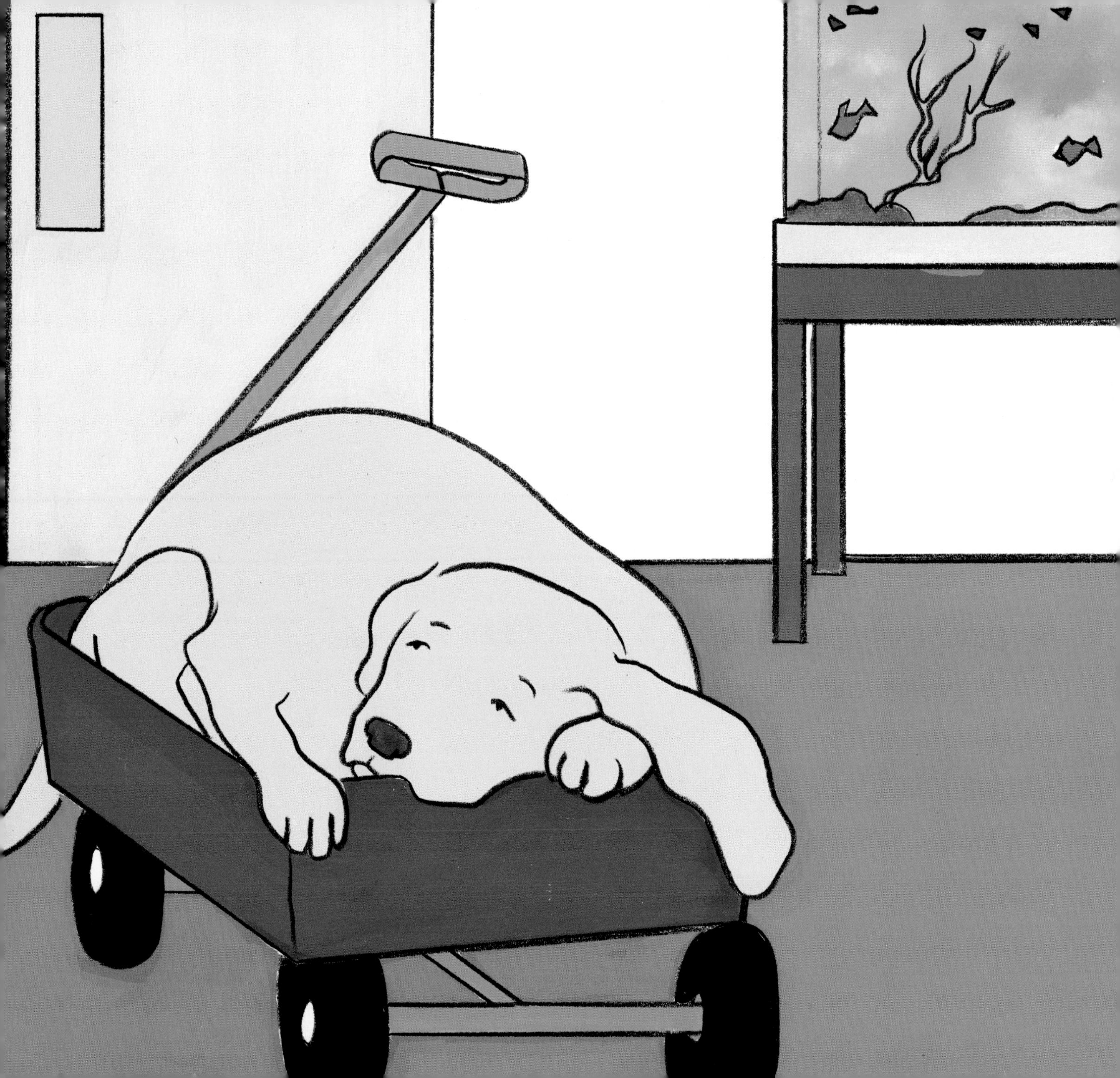

Dr. Phelp
had to help.

Hunky Dory
ate it.

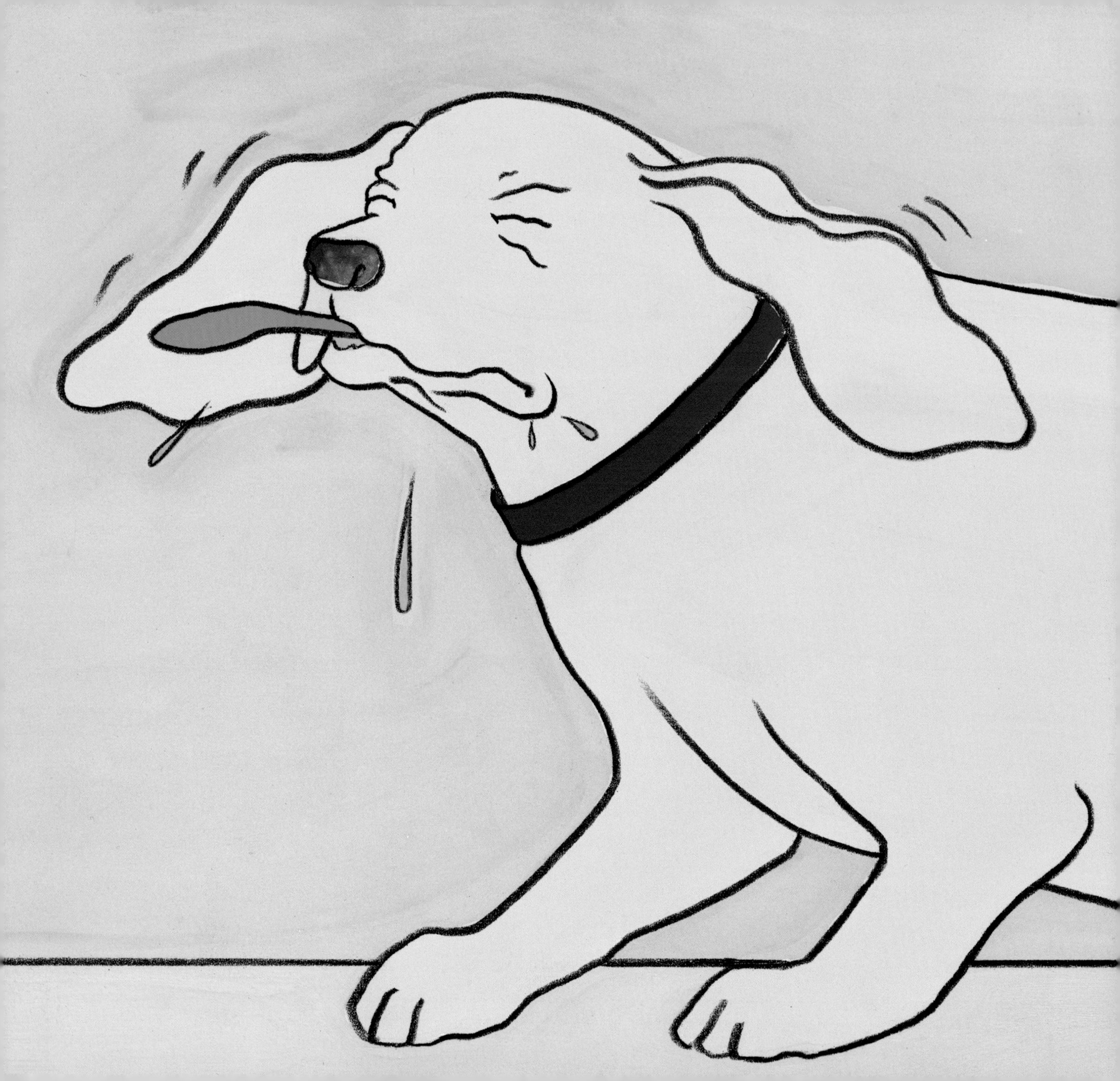

Hunky Dory hated it.

PUFFIN UNICORN BOOKS
Published by the Penguin Group
Penguin Books USA Inc., 375 Hudson Street, New York, New York 10014, U.S.A.
Penguin Books Ltd, 27 Wrights Lane, London W8 5TZ, England
Penguin Books Australia Ltd, Ringwood, Victoria, Australia
Penguin Books Canada Ltd, 10 Alcorn Avenue, Toronto, Ontario, Canada M4V 3B2
Penguin Books (N.Z.) Ltd, 182-190 Wairau Road, Auckland 10, New Zealand
Penguin Books Ltd, Registered Offices: Harmondsworth, Middlesex, England

Library of Congress number 91-13992
ISBN 0-14-055856-X
Published in the United States by Dutton Children's Books,
a division of Penguin Books USA Inc.
Designer: Riki Levinson
Printed in Hong Kong by South China Printing Co.
First Puffin Unicorn Edition 1996
1 3 5 7 9 10 8 6 4 2

HUNKY DORY ATE IT is also available in hardcover
from Dutton Children's Books.